MASTERS OF THE UNIVERSE™

TIME TROUBLE

by ROGER McKENZIE
illustrated by LUIS EDUARDO BARRETO

A GOLDEN BOOK • NEW YORK
Western Publishing Company, Inc., Racine, Wisconsin 53404

1 J

It was a long, lazy day in Eternia—the very kind that Prince Adam liked best—or *would* have, if not for Teela!

"We *all* have work to do," she said. "Even Orko is practicing his magic. Are you going to lie there forever?"

"No," Adam yawned.
"Just until lunchtime."

"Why can't you be *more* like
He-Man?" Teela asked, dumping
Adam to the ground.
"He's a *real* hero!"

"It's too bad," Orko chuckled, "that she doesn't know the *truth* about 'lazy' Prince Adam."

"It's enough that *you* do," Adam said, dusting himself off. "Remember Orko, you're sworn to secrecy about my identity."

Suddenly a falcon flew past—a *special* falcon.

"ZOAR!" Adam exclaimed. "The Sorceress of Castle Grayskull in her falcon form! Something must be wrong!"

Prince Adam drew his hidden
sword. "By the Power of
Grayskull!" he shouted.
Magic coursed along the blade
like lightning. It enveloped
Adam and his pet tiger Cringer.

The magic from the Sword of Power changed Prince Adam and Cringer into He-Man and Battle Cat—two of Eternia's greatest champions!

"Some trick," Orko mumbled as his cards scattered.

To *Castle* Grayskull!

Riding Battle Cat, He-Man followed Zoar to Castle Grayskull. He charged across the Jaw Bridge and entered the castle.

Once inside the dark and mysterious castle, Zoar changed back into the Sorceress. "There is great danger," she told He-Man.

I wonder what the trouble is?

The Sorceress gestured magically. "This is the Eye of Eternia. It can reveal *any* foe in any dimension—even Skeletor. But it is not without risk."

"To stop that evil Lord of Destruction," said He-Man, "I would risk anything!"

The Eye of Eternia opened to show a terrible sight.

"It is *worse* than I'd dreamed!" the Sorceress exclaimed. "Skeletor and his evil followers have passed into another dimension and have found the Cosmic Clock! With it, The Lord of Destruction can control time!"

Skeletor seemed to *sense* that he was being watched. He looked back through the Eye at the heroes.

What foul magic is this?

He-Man! I need your help!

Skeletor struck with all his evil magic. Dark arms leaped from the Eye of Eternia like serpents. One arm twisted around He-Man. Another of the foul arms snaked toward Battle Cat. The Sorceress threw up a magical shield before her, but several arms spilled around its edges!

He-Man tried to save the Sorceress, but he was too late. She was pulled *into* the Eye of Eternia, and brought to the dark and mysterious dimension where Skeletor was waiting to take her prisoner!

No! Sorceress! I have failed, Battle Cat. She is gone!

Meanwhile, Orko was entertaining the royal court of Eternia. "Behold," he exclaimed with a grand sweep of his arm, "the wizardry of Orko the Magnificent!"

"A floating house of cards," applauded King Randor.

"Marvelous," said Queen Marlena.

Suddenly He-Man rushed in, carrying the Eye of Eternia. "No time for parlor tricks now, Orko," he said. "We need *real* magic!" He proceeded to tell of the events at Castle Grayskull. "With the Sorceress captured, you are our only hope," said He-Man. "Your magic is the one thing that can save her!"

"Can you work this, Orko?" He-Man asked, pointing to the Eye.

"W-Wouldn't you rather have me pull a rabbit from a helmet?" Orko stammered. "Th-that's more my style."

"The Sorceress needs your help," said He-Man. "We must not let her down!"

"Well," Orko said timidly, "here goes nothing!"

"No," growled Battle Cat, "here goes *everything*!"

There was a flash of magic as He-Man and his friends disappeared into the Eye of Eternia.

"I hope you know what you're doing," King Randor said.

THOOM!

He-Man and his allies soon found themselves in a dark and nameless dimension. They were face-to-face with Skeletor and his evil companions—Beast Man, Mer-Man, and Evil-Lyn! The Sorceress was in a glass prison.

"Too late, He-Man," Skeletor boasted. "I've got the Sorceress *and* the Cosmic Clock!"

The Sorceress spoke directly into He-Man's
mind. "You must stop Skeletor," she said.
"If the Cosmic Clock strikes twelve, it will give the Dark Lord
the power to control time! If that happens, we are all doomed!"

And so the battle began.

Battle Cat freed the Sorceress
from the mystic cage.
He-Man pitted his strength
against Skeletor's sorcery.

The Cosmic Clock struck nine,
and then ten. Time was
running out!

BONG
BONG

The Cosmic Clock pealed for the eleventh time!

"You have lost, He-Man," Skeletor hissed. "When the Cosmic Clock strikes but once more, I will control time—and all Eternia will feel my fury!"

BONG

"NEVER!" He-Man shouted as he grabbed the huge pendulum. He held it back to stop it from striking for the final time!

There was a terrible explosion. The heroes lost sight of each other and of their enemies.

He-Man and his friends found themselves safely back at the Palace of Eternia.

"Good thing I kept an...uh...*eye* on you," Orko said. "How was that for a last-second rescue?"

"Splendid," He-Man said. "The Sorceress is free, and Skeletor's plan to control time has failed!"

Orko took a bow in front of his floating house of cards—which was finished at last. "I knew I could do it," he said.

But when Orko bowed, he bumped into the cards!

Orko floated in mid-air wearing a silly grin. His house of cards was scattered all around him.

"So the great magician cannot even do a simple card trick!" He-Man taunted.

In light of Orko's recent display of magical skill, everyone found this quite amusing.